The Dead Sea Squirrels Series

Squirreled Away

Boy Meets Squirrels

Nutty Study Buddies

Squirrelnapped!

Tree-mendous Trouble

Whirly Squirrelies

Merle of Nazareth

A Dusty Donkey Detour

Jingle Squirrels

D0951564

Boy Meets Squirrels

Mike Nawrocki

Illustrated by Luke Séguin-Magee

Tyndale House Publishers
Carol Stream, Illinois

Visit Tyndale's website for kids at tyndale.com/kids.

Visit the author's website at mikenawrocki.com.

TYNDALE is a registered trademark of Tyndale House Ministries. The Tyndale Kids logo is a trademark of Tyndale House Ministries.

The Dead Sea Squirrels is a registered trademark of Michael L. Nawrocki.

Boy Meets Squirrels

Designed by Libby Dykstra

Edited by Sarah Rubio

Published in association with the literary agency of Brentwood Studios, 1550 McEwen, Suite 300 PNB 17, Franklin, TN 37067.

Scripture quotations are taken from the *Holy Bible*, New Living Translation, copyright © 1996, 2004, 2015 by Tyndale House Foundation. Used by permission of Tyndale House Publishers, Inc., Carol Stream, Illinois 60188. All rights reserved.

Boy Meets Squirrels is a work of fiction. Where real people, events, establishments, organizations, or locales appear, they are used fictitiously. All other elements of the novel are drawn from the author's imagination.

For manufacturing information regarding this product, please call 1-855-277-9400.

For information about special discounts for bulk purchases, please contact Tyndale House Publishers at csresponse@tyndale.com, or call 1-855-277-9400.

Library of Congress Cataloging-in-Publication Data
Names: Nawrocki, Michael, author.
Title: Boy meets squirrels / Mike Nawrocki.
Description: Carol Stream, Illinois : Tyndale House Publishers, Inc., [2019]
  | Series: Dead sea squirrels | Summary: Will Michael heed the advice of his
  2,000-year-old squirrel souvenirs from the Dead Sea, or, in his attempt to
  get revenge, will he become a bully himself?
Identifiers: LCCN 2018037428 | ISBN 9781496435026 (sc)
Subjects: | CYAC: Bullies—Fiction. | Revenge—Fiction. | Schools—Fiction.
  | Squirrels—Fiction. | Christian life—Fiction.
Classification: LCC PZ7.N185 Bo 2019 | DDC [Fic]—dc23 LC record available
  at https://lccn.loc.gov/2018037428

Printed in the United States of America

27   26   25   24   23   22
9   8   7   6   5   4

To my wife, Lisa—
Thank you for not letting me not pursue this
idea. Your persistent encouragement kept
the squirrels preserved for many years.
I love you.

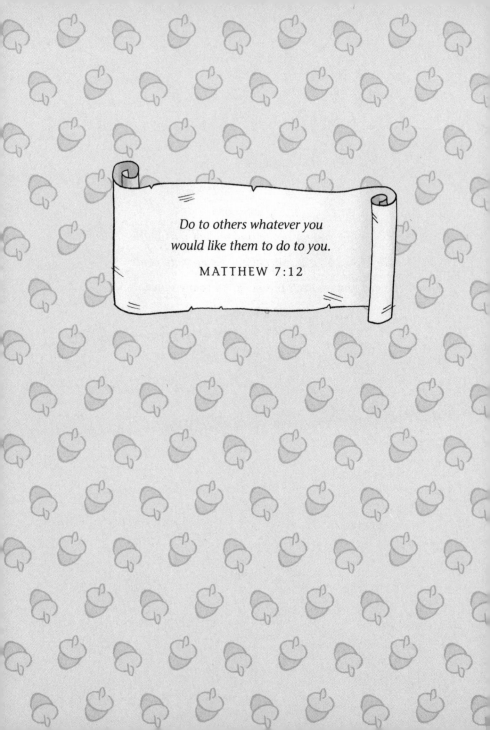

*Do to others whatever you
would like them to do to you.*

MATTHEW 7:12

BUT WAIT!

BEFORE WE START...

Who are the Dead Sea Squirrels?

ISRAEL, AD 70

Merle and Pearl cruise down the Jordan River...

...on the vacation of a lifetime!

The squirrels end up at the Dead Sea, where...

You can't sink! I've always wanted to not sink!

Couldn't you have just worn your floaties in the lake back home?

Soon the two salty squirrels are hot, thirsty, and desperate for shade. Then they spot a cave.

If God wanted you to go into a cave, he would have made you a bat.

Merle's sense of adventure lures him into the cave, despite Pearl's protests.

Ten-year-old Michael Gomez is spending the summer at the Dead Sea with his professor dad and his best friend, Justin.

While exploring a cave (without his dad's permission), Michael discovers two dried-out, salt-covered critters and stashes them in his backpack.

Michael sneaks the squirrels back home with him to Tennessee.

He sets them up like posable action figures on his dresser— under an open window.

While Michael is sleeping, a thunderstorm rolls in, and it begins to rain . . .

. . . rehydrating the squirrels!

Up and kicking again after almost 2,000 years, Merle and Pearl Squirrel have great stories and advice to share with the modern world.

They are the Dead Sea Squirrels!

CHAPTER 1

The bell sounded, and so ended the first day of fifth grade.

"One down, 179 to go!" Michael Gomez said as he closed his history textbook and packed it into his homeroom desk.

"Don't rush it!" Michael's best friend, Justin, said, standing up from his desk and slinging on his backpack. "We're fifth graders for a whole year. Elementary school royalty! Enjoy it!"

"Yeah, I guess you're right," Michael replied as they headed into

the hallway. "Next year, we'll be back down at the bottom of the pile again in middle school."

Justin stopped an unsuspecting second grader in the hall. "You there, young one. Would you like some wise advice from an older and much, much wiser fifth grader?"

"Um . . . I gotta go." The kid hurried away.

"He's obviously intimidated by our greatness," Michael said. "Have you seen Sadie today? I want to tell her about the squirrels."

"Nope. Haven't seen her."

"You gotta come check them out. I set them up in cool poses on my dresser. They look like crusty action figures."

3

"Gross," Justin replied. He was not a fan of the two petrified squirrels Michael had brought home from their summer trip. The friends had spent the whole summer in a tent near the Dead Sea in the Middle East with Michael's dad, who was a professor of ancient civilizations. On the last day of their trip, Michael nearly got lost forever when he disappeared into a cave, all by himself, to retrieve the disgusting little creatures.

"*Gross* is just the word that came to mind when I saw you coming!" a voice called out as Michael and Justin exited the school to cut through the playground on their walk home. Edgar, by far the biggest kid at school, leaned against the jungle gym with two smaller fourth-grade friends who seemed to think Edgar's comment was hilarious.

"Hey, Edgar," Justin answered nervously. One of the reasons Edgar was the biggest kid in school was that he was most likely the oldest. No one had ever dared to ask him how old he was,

but Michael and Justin were pretty sure he had to be at least 12. Even though he was only in fourth grade, everyone knew rule number one at Walnut Creek Elementary School was Don't Mess with Edgar.

But now Michael was elementary school royalty. He stuck out his chest. "Don't mess with us, Edgar. We're fifth graders!"

Terrified, Justin whispered to Michael, "What did you say?"

Not terrified in the least, Edgar stepped forward and yelled, "WHAT DID YOU SAY?!"

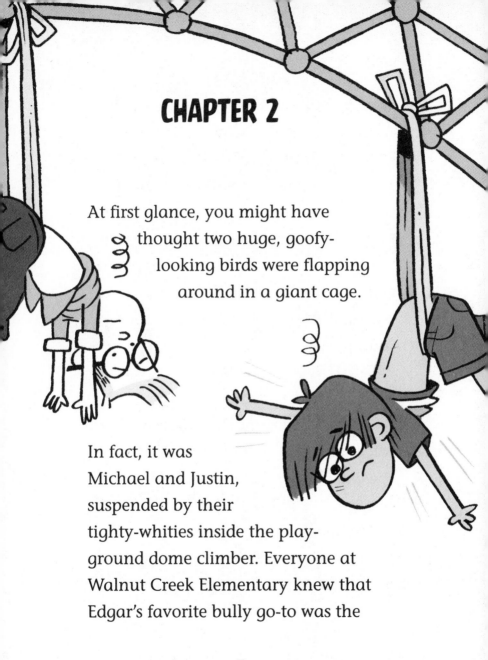

CHAPTER 2

At first glance, you might have thought two huge, goofy-looking birds were flapping around in a giant cage.

In fact, it was Michael and Justin, suspended by their tighty-whities inside the playground dome climber. Everyone at Walnut Creek Elementary knew that Edgar's favorite bully go-to was the wedgie, but he always made a point of finding creative ways to use it.

"Edgar, you are a wedgie artist!" commented Pete, one of the smaller fourth graders.

"Let's get out of here!" Edgar said to his two minions. "Hope you two don't mind if we don't HANG OUT with you!" He laughed. His buddies laughed even louder.

"HAHAHA!" they belted out as they walked away proudly.

"Help!" Justin shouted as he and Michael dangled helplessly above the wood chips. "Get us out of here!"

Michael hung in midair, arms folded. "We are fifth graders now," he fumed. "This can't be happening."

"It obviously is," Justin replied. "Edgar is still bigger, even though he's a grade behind us."

"Yeah, but we're smarter!" Michael shouted.

"Are we?" Justin asked. "Are we?!"

"If we don't make Edgar pay for this, it's going to ruin everything for fifth graders everywhere forever."

"What do you mean, 'make Edgar pay for this'?" Justin asked. "Also, what do you mean, 'we'?"

"I mean revenge." Michael twisted around, trying to unhook himself from the climber. "Remember when we built that water balloon launcher out of rubber tubes and a funnel? Imagine Edgar getting off the bus in the morning and, *WHAM!* A water balloon right in the face! He's soaked all day!"

Justin shook his head. "We'd get suspended, or Edgar would kill us, or both."

"There's got to be something we can do with bees," Michael pondered.

"The flying, stinging kind?" Justin asked.

"Yes. Bees." Michael tapped his fingertips together like a supervillain.

"You're nuts." Justin turned his back on Michael and called out again, "HEEEEELLLP!"

CHAPTER 3

"Oh hey, guys. How was your summer?"

Michael and Justin turned to see their friend Sadie exiting the school. The three of them had been friends since kindergarten and were almost always together. Sadie was still a little hurt that she hadn't been invited to go with Michael and Justin on their summer adventure, so while she hadn't exactly been trying to avoid them all day, she hadn't been trying too hard to find them either.

"Aren't you going to ask us why we're hanging from the monkey bars by our underwear?" Michael asked.

"That's clearly Edgar's work." Sadie tilted her head to the side. "I've got to say, the kid's a wedgie artist."

"Yeah, well, we'll see what kind of artist he is when he finds his backpack filled with earthworms," Michael said.

"Huh?" Sadie frowned.

"He's plotting revenge," Justin said. He turned to Michael. "What happened to the bees?"

14

"I remembered that I'm afraid of bees."

"Revenge is never a good idea," Sadie said. "Well, nice seeing you guys."

"What?! Where are you going?" Michael yelled. "Aren't you going to help us?!"

Sadie put her hands on her hips. "Oh, so I'm good enough to help you but not good enough to invite on your trip?"

"I explained to you like a million times I could only invite one friend, and I needed to share a tent. I wish you could have gone too," Michael said.

Hearing this made Sadie feel a little better.

Michael squirmed. "Help us down, and we'll tell you all about it! Plus, I've

got something super cool to show both
of you guys."

"All right." Sadie climbed to the top
of the monkey bar dome and untied
the two white elastic bows that held
the boys in place.

"UGH!"

"OOF!"

Michael and Justin hit the wood
chips in a cloud of splinters.

CHAPTER 4

"You went back into the cave by yourself in the middle of the night? What
is wrong with you?" Sadie exclaimed
as the friends headed toward Michael's
house. All three lived close enough to
school to walk on nice days,
and this was a beauti-
ful day. However,
Michael and Justin
had long since
made the deci-
sion to walk to
and from school
even on not-so-
nice days, even
on horrible days

when the rain blew sideways or giant icicles fell from the sky. Walking to school meant you didn't have to take the bus, and not taking the bus meant steering clear of Edgar.

"I know, I know—it wasn't the best idea I've ever had," Michael admitted. "But wait until you see what I found."

"It's pretty disgusting," Justin said.

"Shhhhh! Don't say anything, Justin!" Michael said. "You both have to promise not to tell anyone what you're about to see."

"I know what I'm about to see, so threatening to not show me if I don't promise doesn't make any sense," Justin pointed out.

"Will you just promise already?" Michael demanded.

Justin thought for a moment, then shrugged and said, "All right. I promise."

"I'm not interested in seeing something disgusting," Sadie said.

"That's just Justin's opinion. You're gonna think it's the coolest thing ever." The trio arrived at Michael's house. He paused before opening the door and looked at Sadie. "So do you promise?"

"Okay, okay, I promise," Sadie replied. Michael pushed open the door, and they went inside.

CHAPTER 5

Michael stood in his doorway, shocked. "Where did they go?!" He rushed over to his dresser, where he had last seen the squirrels. "Maybe they fell on the floor? Or out the window?" He frantically searched the area around the dresser and leaned out the window to check the ground below. Nothing. "Mom! Did you clean my room?" he shouted at the top of his lungs. In some families, when you want to talk to a family member, you go to the room where they are. Other families have fancy intercom systems that broadcast your voice across the house at the touch of a button. The preferred method of long-distance communication in the Gomez household was to yell. Loudly.

"No!" Mrs. Gomez's muffled yell came through the wall.

"You lost them already?" Justin asked.

"Lost what?" said Sadie.

"Mr. Nemesis!" Michael ran out of his room.

Sadie looked confused. "He lost his cat?"

"No, not his cat," Justin replied, following Michael out.

"Would somebody please tell me what is going on?" Sadie followed her friends out of the room. "Michael!" she shouted.

"I think he lost something," said a small voice from inside the room

next to Michael's. Sadie popped her
head into the room. Jane, Michael's
four-year-old sister, was sitting on her
bed, tying a bonnet onto the head of
Mr. Nemesis, the family cat.

"Oh hi, Jane. Do you know what
he's looking for?" Sadie asked.

"Nope. Do you like Mr. Nemesis's
hat?" Jane said.

"Meow," said Mr.
Nemesis, in a very
annoyed tone of
cat voice.

"It's so cute!"
Sadie said.
"Well, it's defi-
nitely not the
cat that's lost."
She continued
down the hall

and into the living room. "Michael!"
she called out again.

"In the basement!" she heard Michael
yell through the floor.

As Sadie headed toward the basement stairs, a quick movement caught
her eye from the direction of the
couch. She turned her head toward
it but saw nothing. *What was that?*

She walked over to the couch and knelt down to look underneath. Suddenly, she noticed another quick motion to her right and heard the distinct pitter-patter of little paws. She turned quickly to see the door to the laundry room moving ever so slightly. *Did something just run into the laundry room?*

"Come down and help us look!" Justin's voice said through the floor.

"Hold on a second!" Sadie crept slowly toward the laundry room, her eyes fixed on the door opening. Cautiously, she cracked the door open just enough to fit her head through. For a moment, everything was perfectly still. Then she noticed the slightest bit of motion on a towel hanging out of a laundry hamper. She tiptoed toward the basket.

"Sometimes Mr. Nemesis likes to hide things," Sadie heard Michael say as he opened the door to the laundry room.

"Shhhhh!" Sadie put her finger over her lips. With the same finger, she then pointed toward the laundry hamper.

Justin entered the laundry room. "What are—?"

"Shhhhh!" Sadie shushed louder.
"There's something in the hamper,"
she whispered.

"Why are you whispering?" Michael whispered as the three friends huddled around the laundry hamper. Sadie lifted the lid slowly. As light poured into the basket, the three friends peeked inside.

"AHHHHH!" screamed two tiny voices from within the hamper.

"AHHHHH!" screamed Sadie, Michael, and Justin.

CHAPTER 6

"So, you brought these cute little guys back home with you from the Dead Sea?" Sadie asked. The three had managed to smuggle the squirrels from the laundry room past Michael's mom, Jane, and Mr. Nemesis. The squirrels, Merle and Pearl, sat on the bed looking disoriented and frightened as Michael, Justin, and Sadie stood huddled around them.

"Yeah, but they were . . . dead," Justin said.

"These are definitely not dead squirrels," Sadie responded.

Merle nodded slightly, but he got a quick elbow jab and a "shush" look from Pearl.

"They were . . . crusty," Michael said. "I don't get it. I set them up like squirrel-jerky action figures." He posed just like he had posed Merle.

"What do you mean, 'crusty'?" Sadie asked.

"Crusty, like crusty," Michael answered.

"They were stiff as boards, and their fur was covered in salt." He walked over to his dresser. "I put them right here, all dead and stiff, and now *this*. I don't get it!"

"They didn't move at all when you found them in the cave?" Justin asked.

At the word *cave*, Merle brightened as his memory of getting lost in the cave came back to him. He looked to Pearl, who nodded slightly at him. She remembered too.

"Nope. Not an inch. Not in the cave, not in my backpack, not on the plane," Michael said.

"That's so weird," Sadie said.

"Yep. I never saw them move either." Justin frowned at the squirrels.

Merle, who was not much for staying quiet, said, "Maybe it was the rain?"

The three kids turned their heads slowly toward Merle, who shrugged.

"AHHHHH!" they screamed.

"Merle!" Pearl whisper-yelled. "I told you to keep quiet!"

"AHHHHH!" the kids screamed again.

CHAPTER 7

"I have no idea where we are, but wherever it is, the people here sure do like to yell," Merle said to Pearl.

He turned to the kids. "What's wrong? Never heard a squirrel talk before?"

The kids all slowly shook their heads in response.

"Merle, you're scaring the children. They've obviously never heard a squirrel talk," Pearl said. "It's okay," she told the three friends. "Don't be afraid. We don't bite. Well, we do bite, but not children. Mostly just nuts."

"And the occasional insect," added Merle. "Not my favorite, but when nuts are scarce, what are you gonna do?" He shrugged.

The kids stared at the squirrels, not believing their own ears. "Um," Michael finally said, "we've never heard a squirrel talk."

"Nope," Sadie and Justin confirmed.

Now that the shock of meeting the kids was wearing off, Merle didn't feel shy at all. "So, I've been thinking about this," he said. "The last thing I remember is Pearl and me getting lost in a cave."

"I told you not to go in there," Pearl reminded him.

"I know, I know, and I should have listened to you, Paul, Moses, and God, but here we are," Merle said. "By the way, thanks for rescuing us," he said to Michael. "Any idea how long we were in there?"

Michael shook his head.

"From the looks of things, the world's a different place since we entered that cave." Pearl gazed around the room.

"I know!" Merle exclaimed. "It's wonderful! Who would imagine a bowl that never runs out of water no matter how much you drink?!" Merle motioned toward Michael's bathroom.

"I was parched when I woke up.
Couldn't get enough!"

"Ewww," Sadie whispered to Justin.
"I think he drank out of the toilet."

"And so fresh!" Merle continued.

"Yeah, it's probably not that fresh," Justin said.

"We were all dried out and super salty . . . I'm thinking we could have kept for a good long time in that condition, like they do with fish!" Merle guessed.

"Fish are dead before that point," Pearl pointed out.

"Maybe squirrels can go on kicking!" Merle stood up tall and stuck his chest out. "Squirrels are survivors! So when we got wet from the rain blowing in last night, we started back up again!"

"Whoa," Michael said. It was better than any explanation he could think

of, and maybe the only plausible one.
"But . . . how can you . . . talk?"

Merle and Pearl looked at each other
and shrugged. "We've always been
able to," Pearl said.

"To . . . people?" Sadie questioned.

"Among others," Merle answered. "By the way, I'm Merle, and this is my lovely wife, Pearl."

Pearl bowed with her paw over her heart. "Pleased to meet you."

"Um, I'm Michael, and these are my friends Justin and Sadie."

"Nice to meet you, Michael, Justin, and Sadie!" Merle said cheerfully. "Now, we're starving. Anybody got any nuts?"

CHAPTER 8

KNOCK, KNOCK, KNOCK! Someone was at Michael's door. Michael looked from the squirrels to his friends in panic. *What if it's Mom? She would totally freak out!* he thought. He grabbed a folded blanket from the foot of his bed and flung it over the squirrels.

"Hey!" complained Merle.

"Shhhhh!" Michael hushed. "Who is it?" he called out nervously.

"What are you guys doing?" asked Jane through the door.

Michael relaxed slightly and cracked open the door to pop his head out. "Nothing."

Mr. Nemesis, still wearing the ridiculous baby bonnet Jane had dressed him in, took the opportunity to slip into the room.

"No!" Michael chased after the cat as it headed to his backpack on the floor. Mr. Nemesis was curious if the scent from the night before was still there.

Sniff, sniff. There was just a hint of the scent on the bag. Mr. Nemesis looked around the room suspiciously as Michael scooped him up and brought him back to the doorway.

"Please keep your cat out of my room." Michael handed Mr. Nemesis to Jane and closed the door.

"The bonnet still looks great!" Sadie called out to Jane as the door clicked shut.

"Thank you!" Jane said cheerfully through the door.

"Meow," Mr. Nemesis said grumpily.

Michael looked at his friends. "You

guys, we can't leave the squirrels here during the day. Jane only goes to pre-school three days a week, and she'll be home on Monday."

"What else are you going to do with them?" Justin asked.

"I share a room with my sister," Sadie said. "I can't keep them."

"Do we have any say in the matter?" Pearl called out from under the blanket.

"Oh! Sorry!" Michael took the blanket off the squirrels.

Merle brushed blanket lint from his fur. "Not a

fan of confined, dark spaces after our latest adventure," he said.

"Sorry, Merle," Michael said. "But we can't let Jane, or Mr. Nemesis, or anyone know about you."

"Why not?" asked Merle.

"Um . . ." Michael thought about it. "I don't know. I'm just sure it would mean trouble."

"What are we gonna do, then?" Justin asked.

Michael shrugged. "All I know is that I can't leave them here while I'm gone."

"So where will they go when you're in class?" asked Sadie.

Michael looked over at his backpack, then took a deep breath and said, "I guess I'm taking them to school."

CHAPTER 9

"It's so green here! Look at all the trees!" Pearl marveled, her head poking out of Michael's backpack as she and Merle rode along on Michael and Justin's walk to school. Sadie was riding the bus. Edgar never messed with her. "Is it always this green?"

"Not in the winter," Michael replied.

"Squirrel!" Merle shouted, pointing at a neighborhood squirrel perched on a branch of a walnut tree. "Good morning, brother!" The tree squirrel did not answer, but he seemed to understand Merle. He waved his paw as if to say hello and swiped his tail at a large walnut sitting on the branch next to him.

The walnut flew off the branch and into Merle's paws. "Thank you, kind squirrel!" Merle said.

"I think I could really grow to like this place," Pearl said as she and Merle dropped down into the backpack to enjoy the walnut. "It's so pretty, and everyone is so nice!"

"Well, well, well, if it isn't the monkey bar brothers!" a familiar voice called out from the street. Michael and Justin looked up to see the school bus approaching them, with Edgar's head sticking out of one of the windows. "I hope you had fun hanging out!"

Edgar's two minions stuck their heads out of the window next to him, and they all laughed hysterically as the bus zipped by Michael and Justin and turned into the school parking lot. "HAHAHAHAHA! Fourth graders rule!!!!!"

"Not everyone is so nice," Michael said to Pearl. He turned to Justin. "With keeping the squirrels hidden all weekend, I forgot about our plan."

"Just drop it, Michael," Justin said. "You've got more important things to worry about—like making sure Mr. P. doesn't find the squirrels." As the principal of Walnut Creek Elementary School, Mr. P. ran a tight ship, and he definitely didn't allow kids to bring their pets to school. "Remember when Marlowe brought her ferret?"

"Oh yeah." Michael smiled, remembering how Abbott the ferret had hidden Mr. P.'s car keys. "That was awesome."

"Yeah, it was awesome, but Marlowe got a month of detention."

"Don't worry. Nobody's gonna find the squirrels. Right, guys?" Michael called to Merle and Pearl, hidden snugly in his backpack.

"Nrppp," Merle said, his mouth stuffed with walnut.

The boys arrived at school and headed to their classroom. "We'll talk at lunch, Justin," Michael said. We've got payback to plan!"

TURBO SHARPENER
7000

CHAPTER 10

When you're a squirrel from the Middle
East who's been frozen in time for who
knows how long, a fifth-grade classroom in modern-day middle Tennessee
can be a fascinating place. Merle spent
the morning peeking out of Michael's
backpack, oohing and ahhing at all
the amazing gadgets around him,
while Pearl tried her best to keep him
from being seen. From pencil sharpen-
ers to smart boards to the teacher's lap-
top computer, Merle had no idea what
all this stuff was and what it did, but
he was very interested in finding out.
After all, he was a squirrel who was
good with his paws, and he'd enjoyed

building things ever since he was a kit. He'd built the raft that had carried him and Pearl down the Jordan River to the Dead Sea. And while you could argue that the Dead Sea was not the best place in the world for two squirrels to vacation, there was no denying that it had been a fine raft, a fact Merle constantly reminded Pearl of.

"Pearl!" Merle whispered. "Look at that contraption on the wall. The kids put a dull stick in, and it makes a kind of strange chewing noise. After a few seconds, it comes out a sharp stick!"

"I don't see why a stick sharpener is necessary," Pearl said.

"Are you kidding me? I could build tons of stuff with sharp sticks!" Merle exclaimed.

"Like what?"

"I don't know specifically at the moment, but I could figure something out."

"Shhhhh!" Pearl shushed her husband. "Keep your voice down."

"I'm telling you, Pearl, this place is amazing!" Merle whispered. "If I hadn't gotten us lost in that cave, we would have never found this place! You're welcome."

Pearl sniffed. "If it means spending every day in a backpack, I'm not ready to thank you, Merle."

"True." Merle poked his head out of the backpack. "Pssssst! Michael! When's lunch?"

Michael looked around, terrified that someone might have heard or seen Merle. Thankfully, no one had. "Soon!" Michael whispered. "Now get down and be quiet!"

CHAPTER 11

"Okay, guys, what are we gonna do to Edgar?" Michael said as he plopped down his tray of chicken nuggets.

"We?" said Sadie. "Don't bring me into this."

"How did he get so big?" Justin wondered nervously as he looked across the lunchroom at Edgar, who was sitting next to his two cronies at the fourth-grade table. "I mean, he'd be huge even for an eighth grader."

"If nobody else has any ideas, I thought of one that involves a tree, a bus, and a bucket of goo," Michael said.

"Does it also involve getting destroyed by Edgar?" Justin asked.

Sadie nodded. "That would be a yes."

"Be brave, Justin!" Michael said. "This is bigger than us. We're doing this for fifth graders everywhere! Vengeance will be ours!"

"I really wish you would stop saying *we*," Sadie said.

"Excuse me." Merle popped out of Michael's backpack, holding a half-eaten chicken nugget. "These are AMAZING!! What do you call these things?"

"Chicken nuggets," Michael said.

"The next time I see any chickens, I will thank them for their nuggets." Merle finished off his nugget and grabbed another.

"Do you two have any ideas for an epic prank?" Michael asked the squirrels.

"Prank?" Pearl questioned.

"Yeah, something we can do to

really embarrass Edgar, this kid who's always humiliating us," Michael replied.

"Like revenge?" Merle asked.

"Yep!" Michael smiled. "I want to give Edgar a taste of his own medicine!"

Pearl frowned. "Revenge is never a good idea."

"See? That's exactly what I said!" Sadie tried to give Pearl a fist bump. Pearl, not familiar with the art of the fist bump, simply reached out and patted the top of Sadie's hand.

"Do to others whatever you would like them to do to you," Pearl said.

"Oh! Oh! Sre uh Garrreee!" Merle piped in, his mouth full of nugget.

"What?!" asked Pearl and the kids. Merle gulped down his food and repeated, "Sea of Galilee. I remember that . . ."

CHAPTER 12

"A few years before we got lost in the cave," Pearl said, "Merle and I were looking for walnuts around the Sea of Galilee."

"That's up north from the Dead Sea," Merle added. "And nowhere near as salty."

"We noticed a big crowd gathering on a hillside near the water, so we ran over to see what was going on. The people had come to listen to a teacher," Pearl continued.

"Yep!" said Merle. "He was traveling around the area with his friends, and news got out about what a great teacher he was. There were tons of people. Fortunately for us, we're squirrels, so we had a great treetop view!"

"Most of the people there were poor and had lived very hard lives," Pearl said. "They had been bullied by a group of other people.

The teacher told the crowd that God could bless them. He said, 'God blesses those who are poor and realize their need for him, for the Kingdom of Heaven is theirs.'"

"There were lots of blessings," Merle said. "But I also remember him saying, 'God blesses those who are merciful, for they will be shown mercy.' And 'God blesses those who work for peace, for they will be called the children of God.'"

"Good memory, Merle!" Pearl complimented.

"God blesses with good memory those who eat a lot of walnuts . . . I made that one up," Merle confessed.

"The teacher had a lot of other things to say, but one thing that I remember very well might help you with Edgar, Michael," said Pearl.

"Was it an idea for an epic prank?" Michael asked.

"Uh, no. He didn't say anything about pranks. He said, 'Do to others whatever you would like them to do to you.'"

"Do to others whatever you would like them to do to you . . . ," Michael repeated. "Huh."

CHAPTER 13

"So," Michael said, "I should be nice to Edgar since I wish Edgar would be nice to me?"

"Exactly!" answered Pearl.

"And since I wouldn't want Edgar to humiliate me, I shouldn't humiliate him?"

"You've got it absolutely right!" replied Pearl. "I'm impressed!"

"Hmm." Michael understood what Pearl was saying, but he didn't like the sound of it. This would ruin his chance for payback.

"Wait. I've heard those words before," Sadie said. She looked at the squirrels for a moment, then asked, "Exactly how long were you in that cave?"

Of course, Merle and Pearl had no way of knowing the answer to that question, but before they could say so, the bell rang and lunch ended.

As the kids were returning to class, Pearl managed to talk Michael into letting her and Merle stay in the lunchroom to "help clean up." Pearl could not believe the amount of food left over from all the kids' lunches, and her instincts told her to make sure to save it. Being a squirrel means never passing up a chance to grab whatever food you can to stash for later.

"Make sure nobody sees you!" Michael warned.

"We'll be stealthy!" Pearl promised. She and Merle then spent the next 30 minutes grabbing every extra chicken nugget, corn cob, French fry, and pizza slice they could get their paws on. The cafeteria workers were pleased that the kids did such a good job finishing their food for once. Little did they know that two squirrels had stuffed nearly every leftover into a 50-gallon trash bag (which Merle swiped from a trash can) right over their heads.

When they were finally alone, high on a light fixture above the clean cafeteria, Pearl said to Merle, "I'm so happy! But how are we going to get this bag down?"

"Easy!" Merle replied as he put a

shoulder to the bag and pushed off
with his back legs. "Gravity!"

The bag of leftovers hit the shiny
linoleum floor with a loud, wet thud.

Merle jumped down next to it. "The
hard part will be getting it home."

CHAPTER 14

Michael spent the entire afternoon devising his scheme. The thought of treating Edgar the way he himself would want to be treated seemed silly. Why would he do that? Edgar didn't deserve it. What he deserved was a taste of his own medicine! When Michael should have been paying attention to Ms. McKay's lesson in long division, he was drawing pulley diagrams and figuring out how much rope, how big of a bucket, and how high of a tree branch he would need to pull off his plan. A few times, Michael passed his drawings to Justin, who was trying his best to concentrate on the lesson. Then Ms. McKay noticed the boys passing notes to each other.

"What is this?" Ms. McKay snatched the paper from Justin's desk.

"Ummm . . ." Justin stammered, terrified that a trip to Principal P.'s office was in his near future.

"Oh! Good work, boys!" Ms. McKay said cheerfully. "It's nice to see you

applying yourselves!" She handed the note back to Justin.

Michael shot Justin a "what just happened?" look. Justin handed Michael back the note. Luckily, Justin had used division to calculate how long it would take a bucket of goo to fall from a 10-foot tree branch onto Edgar's head. Michael smiled and gave Justin a thumbs-up.

Next, when Michael should have been paying attention to the social studies lesson about the Pilgrims, he was trying to figure out what he could use for the goo. *Goo*, as you probably know, is a general term for something slimy and disgusting, but it's not as easy as you might think to find a whole bucket full of it. It would take forever to collect that much worm slime. How much used kitty litter could he get from Mr. Nemesis on such short notice? Soon Michael had a list of crossed-out ideas, none of which had anything to do with the Pilgrims, taking up an entire page of notebook paper. The bell rang.

"Did you figure it all out?" asked Justin.

"Nope. Not yet," Michael answered. "Come on. Let's find Merle and Pearl."

CHAPTER 15

Michael and Justin were very careful to avoid running into Edgar after school. The next time Michael wanted to see him was payback time, which would be just before school tomorrow morning. Michael and Justin slunk back to the cafeteria, hiding behind lockers and doorways to avoid being seen. Entering the cafeteria, they watched through the big glass windows at the front of the lunchroom as Edgar and his pals boarded the afternoon bus.

"The coast is clear!" Michael said. He called out, "Merle? Pearl?"

"Over here!" came a whisper from behind the stack of tables in the corner.

The boys headed over to see Merle and Pearl standing on a large black garbage bag wedged between two tables.

"We need your help getting this home!" Pearl said, pointing to the stuffed-full bag under her paws.

"What is it?" asked Michael.

"Treasure!" Pearl responded with a giddy smile. "Look!" She opened the top of the bag to reveal its contents.

"Ewwww," Justin said. "That's disgusting."

"I beg your pardon," Pearl replied. "This is enough food for a whole year! Do you know how long it normally takes us to find this much food?"

"A whole year," Merle responded. "Obviously."

"I was asking the boy," Pearl said.

"All that food will be completely rotten in no time," Justin said. "There's no way it'll last a year, right, Michael?" Justin looked over to see Michael deep in thought. "Michael?" he asked again.

"Hold my backpack, please," Michael said to Justin. "I got it!"

"You've got what, exactly?" Pearl asked as Michael grabbed the bag and hoisted it up in his arms with a grunt.

Michael headed for the door, straining under the weight of the leftovers. "Let's get this treasure home!"

CHAPTER 16

"What's in the bag?" Sadie asked as she joined Michael, Justin, and the squirrels on their walk home.

"The missing part of my plan!" Michael said.

"Your plan?" Sadie asked.

"He spent all afternoon on it," Justin said.

Michael nodded at his backpack, hanging from Justin's shoulder. "It's in the front pocket of my backpack. Check it out."

Justin pulled the sheets of paper out of Michael's backpack.

THE PLAN!

SUPPLIES

- ☑ Long rope
- ? Slimy goo
- ☑ Big trash can
- ☑ Large tree
- ☑ Long board
- ☑ Duct tape
- ☑ Gravity

LOCATION

Walnut Creek Elementary School
bus drop-off

TIME

Setup time: 7 a.m.

Showtime: 8 a.m.

STEPS

1. Arrive at school at 7 a.m. with all the supplies.

2. Toss rope over big tree branch next to bus stop.

3. Tie trash can full of slimy goo to one end of rope.

4. Hoist trash can full of slimy goo up into tree.

5. Balance slimy goo on branch above bus drop-off area.

6. Duct tape top end of long board to trash can.

7. Position bottom end of long board to be hit by bus door.

8. Bus arrives at 8 a.m.

9. Bus door opens and hits board.

10. Trash can full of slimy goo tips.

11. Edgar exits bus.

12. Slimy goo pours out of trash can and all over Edgar's head!

"Wait. How do you know Edgar will be the first one off the bus?" Sadie asked.

"Edgar's ALWAYS the first one off the bus. Anyone who has ridden the bus with Edgar knows that," Michael said.

"And what's the missing part?" she asked as they arrived at Michael's house.

"The slimy goo!" Michael dumped the contents of the plastic bag into an empty garbage can in the driveway.

"Hey!" Pearl protested.

"Don't worry, Pearl," Michael said, removing a few leftover items for her and Merle. "You won't be able to eat the rest of all this before it spoils." He then grabbed the garden hose and filled up the trash can with water, creating a cold, mucky leftover soup. "By morning, this will have turned into the slimy goo we've been looking for!" He placed a lid on the trash can.

"Stop saying *we*!" Sadie and Justin said.

CHAPTER 17

As the sun rose over Walnut Creek Elementary School, so too did a trash can full of sludge.

Justin inched forward slowly on the ground below with one end of a rope slung over his shoulder, struggling to lift the huge weight and not let the rope slip. "Hrggggg."

"Almost there!" Michael called down to Justin from where he sat on one of the tree's branches, guiding the trash can tied to the other end of the rope. "Just a few more inches!"

Merle and Pearl watched the action from a couple of branches up, concerned.

"Perfect!" Michael said as he wrestled the trash can into position on the branch next to him. After duct-taping the board on as the trigger, the trap was set. "All we have to do now is wait!"

The boys found a comfortable spot in the bushes next to the school with a clear line of sight to the bus drop-off. Michael did not want to miss any of the action.

"You're sure you want to go through with this, huh?" Merle questioned.

"It's not too late," Pearl added.

Michael squirmed. He had thought about Pearl's words quite a bit last night. "Do to others whatever you would like them to do to you." He knew that what he was about to do to Edgar was definitely not what he would like to be done to him.

"Michael!" Justin said. "Look!"

A second grader who had been dropped off early by his mom was poking at the board hanging down from the tree with a stick. "Yikes!" Michael shouted. He ran out of the bushes. "Hold on, kid! Don't go near that!"

"Why not?" the kid asked. "What's it for?"

Michael considered shooing the kid off without an explanation, but looking like a cool fifth grader seemed like a much better idea. "You have to promise not to tell anyone, but I'm going to slime Edgar when he gets off the bus!"

"Wow!" the kid said. "That'll be awesome."

"Yep! It's payback for messing with fifth graders."

"So you're Edgar's bully?" the second grader said.

"What?" Michael asked. "What are you talking about?"

"Edgar bullies a lot of kids—so you're the one who bullies him!" the kid said.

Michael's heart sank. *I'm no bully*, he thought. *I don't like being bullied, so why would I want to bully someone else?*

GRRRRRURRRGGG! The sound of a bus engine interrupted Michael's thoughts. He turned to see Edgar's bus pulling into the school.

"Do to others whatever you would like them to do to you . . . ," Michael said to himself as the bus rolled into the drop-off area. He saw Edgar staring at him through the glass door of the bus—first in line, as always, with his two minions behind him.

"Fourth graders rule!" Edgar shouted.

I can't do this, Michael decided. "Wait! Stop!" he shouted. He waved his arms above his head to signal the bus driver. "Don't open the door!" Unfortunately for Michael, his hand whacked against the trigger board.

SPLURRRRRSHHHHH!!!!! Down came the slimy sludge all over Michael, soaking him from head to toe.

Edgar and his pals had never laughed so hard in their lives.

CHAPTER 18

"You made the right choice," Pearl said from Michael's backpack, which was on the seat next to him at the fifth-grade lunch table.

"I'm still soggy," Michael complained.

"And you smell like old chicken nuggets," Merle added, munching on a newly fried nugget.

"I'm proud of you, Michael," Sadie said. "You didn't become a bully yourself by getting back at Edgar."

Edgar happened to be walking by at that moment. "What?" he said, hearing his name. "Does someone want more garbage dumped on their head?"

"Hahahahaha!" Edgar's friends laughed.

"Nobody's dumping garbage on anyone's head," Justin said firmly, standing up.

"Don't tell me what I can't do," Edgar threatened.

"He's right." Sadie stood up next to Justin. "Nobody's messing with anybody." Michael stood up too, followed by a number of other fifth graders.

Edgar slunk back to the fourth-grade table. "Yeah, never mind," he mumbled, trying to still sound tough. Bullies have a hard time bullying when they are stood up to.

"Merle and Pearl," Sadie said, taking a book out of her backpack, "I found something interesting." She opened the book and put her finger on the page. "'Do to others whatever you would like them to do to you,'" she read. "I knew I had heard those words before. Jesus said them."

"That's right!" Merle said.

"How did you know that?" Pearl asked.

"These words are written in the Bible," Sadie said, showing Merle and Pearl the book.

"Wasn't that written a long time ago?" Michael asked.

"Yeah. Like 2,000 years ago."

"Hold on," said Merle slowly as the truth began to dawn on him. "That

must mean we were in that cave for . . .
for . . . for . . ."

BOOF! Merle fainted, dropping his
half-eaten nugget.

"Oh, my . . . ," Pearl said.

MICHAEL GOMEZ is an adventurous and active 10-year-old boy. He is kindhearted but often acts before he thinks. He's friendly and talkative and blissfully unaware that most of his classmates think he's a bit geeky. Michael is super excited to be in fifth grade, which, in his mind, makes him "grade school royalty!"

MERLE SQUIRREL may be thousands of years old, but he never really grew up. He has endless enthusiasm for anything new and interesting—especially this strange modern world he finds himself in. He marvels at the self-refilling bowl of fresh drinking water (otherwise known as a toilet) and supplements his regular diet of tree nuts with what he believes might be the world's most perfect food: chicken nuggets. He's old enough to know better, but he often finds it hard to do better. Good thing he's got his wife, Pearl, to help him make wise choices.

PEARL SQUIRREL is wise beyond her many, many, many years, with enough common sense for both her and Merle. When Michael's in a bind, she loves to share a lesson or bit of wisdom from Bible events she witnessed in her youth. Pearl's biggest quirk is that she is a nut hoarder. Having come from a world where food is scarce, her instinct is to grab whatever she can. The abundance and variety of nuts in present-day Tennessee can lead to distraction and storage issues.

JUSTIN KESSLER is Michael's best friend. Justin is quieter and has better judgment than Michael, and he is super smart. He's a rule follower and is obsessed with being on time. He'll usually give in to what Michael wants to do after warning him of the likely consequences.

SADIE HENDERSON is Michael and Justin's other best friend. She enjoys video games and bowling just as much as cheerleading and pajama parties. She gets mad respect from her classmates as the only kid at Walnut Creek Elementary who's not afraid of school bully Edgar. Though Sadie's in a different homeroom than her two best friends, the three always sit together at lunch and hang out after class.

DR. GOMEZ, a professor of anthropology, is not thrilled when he finds out that his son, Michael, smuggled two ancient squirrels home from their summer trip to the Dead Sea, but he ends up seeing great value in having them around as original sources for his research. Dad loves his son's adventurous spirit but wishes Michael would look (or at least peek) before he leaps.

MRS. GOMEZ teaches part-time at her daughter's preschool and is a full-time mom to Michael and Jane. She feels sorry for the fish-out-of-water squirrels and looks for ways to help them feel at home, including constructing and decorating an over-the-top hamster mansion for Merle and Pearl in Michael's room. She also can't help but call Michael by her favorite (and his least favorite) nickname, Cookies.

MR. NEMESIS is the Gomez family cat who becomes Merle and Pearl's true nemesis. Jealous of the time and attention given to the squirrels by his family, Mr. Nemesis is continuously coming up with brilliant and creative ways to get rid of them. He hides his ability to talk from the family, but not the squirrels.

JANE GOMEZ is Michael's little sister. She's super adorable but delights in getting her brother busted so she can be known as the "good child." She thinks Merle and Pearl are the cutest things she has ever seen in her whole life (next to Mr. Nemesis) and is fond of dressing them up in her doll clothes.

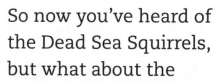

DR. GOMEZ'S
Historical Handbook

So now you've heard of the Dead Sea Squirrels, but what about the **DEAD SEA *SCROLLS*?**

Way back in 1946, just after the end of World War II, in a cave along the banks of the Dead Sea, a 15-year-old boy came across some jars containing ancient scrolls while looking after his goats. When scholars and archaeologists found out about his discovery, the hunt for more scrolls was on! Over the next 10 years, many more scrolls and pieces of scrolls were found in 11 different caves.

There are different theories about exactly who wrote on the scrolls and hid them in the caves. One of the most popular ideas is that they belonged to a group of Jewish priests called Essenes, who lived in the desert because they had been thrown out of Jerusalem. One thing is for sure—the scrolls are very, very old! They were placed in the caves between the years 300 BC and AD 100!

Forty percent of the words on the scrolls come from the Bible. Parts of every Old Testament book except for the book of Esther have been discovered.

Of the remaining 60 percent, half are religious texts not found in the Bible, and half are historical records about the way people lived 2,000 years ago.

The discovery of the Dead Sea Scrolls is one of the most important archaeological finds in history!

About the Author

As co-creator of VeggieTales, co-founder of Big Idea Entertainment, and the voice of the beloved Larry the Cucumber, **MIKE NAWROCKI** has been dedicated to helping parents pass on biblical values to their kids through storytelling for over two decades. Mike currently serves as Assistant Professor of Film and Animation at Lipscomb University in Nashville, Tennessee, and makes his home in nearby Franklin with his wife, Lisa, and their two children. The Dead Sea Squirrels is Mike's first children's book series.

SADDLE UP AND JOIN WINNIE AND HER FAMILY AT THE WILLIS WYOMING RANCH!

Winnie is the star of the bestselling Winnie the Horse Gentler series that sold more than half a million copies and taught kids around the world about faith, kindness, and horse training. Winnie could ride horses before she could walk, but training them is another story. In this new series, eight-year-old Winnie learns the fine art of horse gentling from her horse wrangler mom as they work together to save the family ranch.

www.tyndalekids.com

FOR ADVENTURERS

The Wormling series

Red Rock Mysteries series

FOR COMEDIANS

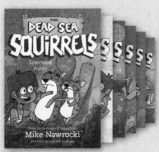

The Dead Sea Squirrels series

FOR ARTISTS

Made to Create with All My
Heart and Soul

Be Bold

FOR ANIMAL LOVERS

Winnie the Horse Gentler series

Starlight Animal Rescue series

CP1337